Walt Disney's Winnie the Pooh
and the Toy Airplane

Written by Joan Phillips
Illustrated by Bill Langley and Russell Schroeder

A Golden Book • New York
Western Publishing Company, Inc., Racine, Wisconsin 53404

Winnie the Pooh
was with
Piglet and Roo.
He saw Tigger.

"Look at my new toy!"
said Tigger.

"Look at it fly!"

"Oh, my," said Pooh.
"How nice!
Do you think that
I could fly IN
your toy?"

"Yes," said Tigger.
"You can fly in it
in a little while.
And you can fly
in it, too, Piglet!"

"Not me,"
said Piglet.
"I do not want
to fly."

"What can we do now?"
said Pooh.

"I know,"
said Piglet.
"We can all look
for pebbles.
I like pebbles.

"Look! Look!"
said Piglet.
"Look at this!"

"Oh, my," said Pooh.
"How nice!"

Roo sat down.
Roo played.
"I am flying!"
he said.

"Oh, my,"
said Roo.
"I am NOT flying!
I am going away!
Help! Help!"

"What did you say, Roo?"
said Pooh.

"Oh, my,"
said Pooh.
"What can we do?"

"Oh, my,"
said Piglet.
"What can we do?"

"Oh, my"
said Roo.
"What can *I* do?"

"We will get you, Roo!"
said Pooh.
"But how?"

"I know,"
said Tigger.
"We can fly to Roo!
You can fly, Pooh!"

Pooh tried to get
in the toy.

"Oh, my," said Pooh.
"What can we do?"

"I know,"
said Tigger.
"Piglet can fly!"

"Not me," said Piglet.
"I do not want
to fly."

"It is up to you,"
said Pooh.
"Oh, my," said Piglet.

Piglet got in the toy.
"Here I go!"
he said.

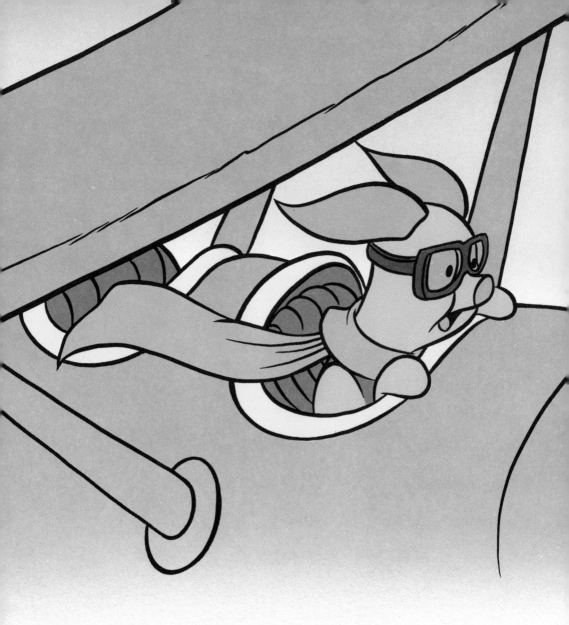

"I am flying!"
said Piglet.

Piglet went to Roo.
Roo got in the toy.
"Here we go!"
said Piglet.
"We are flying!"
said Roo.

"Thank you, Piglet!"
said Pooh, Tigger,
and Roo.
"Here is a pebble, Piglet,"
said Roo.
"Thank YOU!" said Piglet.